D0344033

NEWHAM LIBRARIES

90800101129724

To all children … trust your feelings
JAK

For Oscar
CD

Thank you to the Bank Street Writers Lab
for the support and encouragement. –JAK

First published 2020 by Walker Books Ltd
87 Vauxhall Walk, London SE11 5HJ

10 9 8 7 6 5 4 3 2 1

Text © 2020 Jackie Azúa Kramer
Illustrations © 2020 Cindy Derby

The right of Jackie Azúa Kramer and Cindy Derby to be identified as the
author and illustrator respectively of this work has been asserted by them
in accordance with the Copyright, Designs and Patents Act 1988

This book has been typeset in Berkeley

Printed in China

All rights reserved. No part of this book may be reproduced, transmitted
or stored in an information retrieval system in any form or by any means,
graphic, electronic or mechanical, including photocopying, taping and
recording, without prior written permission from the publisher.

British Library Cataloguing in Publication Data:
a catalogue record for this book is available from the British Library

ISBN 978-1-4063-9554-9

www.walker.co.uk

The Boy and the Gorilla

Jackie Azúa Kramer

illustrated by Cindy Derby

WALKER BOOKS
AND SUBSIDIARIES
LONDON • BOSTON • SYDNEY • AUCKLAND

Your mother's garden is beautiful.

May I help?

OK.

My mum died.

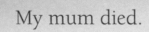

I know.

How do you know when someone dies?

A person's body stops working.

Like their heartbeat?

Yes.

Will we all die?

Yes. We all do. But you have many more kites to fly.

Where did Mum go?

No one knows for sure.

Maybe Mum's here. She liked the waves.

Can't my mum come back home?

No. But she's always with you.

I wish Mum was here
to read to me.

It's a good story.
Your father might like this book, too.

I like Mum's pancakes better.

Sometimes I want to be alone.

That's all right. Everyone needs quiet time.

I'm going to climb to the top!
Maybe Mum will be there!

I'm right behind you.

Why did she have to die?

All living things die. It hurts not to be able to be with someone we love.

When will I feel better?

When you know she's still with you.

Mum and I loved baseball.

That's it. She's with you when you play.

You mean like baking Mum's special biscuits?

Yes, each bite is like a memory.

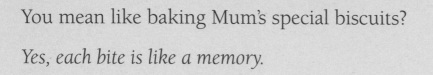

Or picking daisies from Mum's garden?

The seeds you planted together are like your mother's love, a gift to keep forever.

Dad …

I miss Mum.

Mum had a funny laugh.

And she told the best jokes.
I miss your mother, too.

But I can see her in your smile.

Mum will like her new flowers.

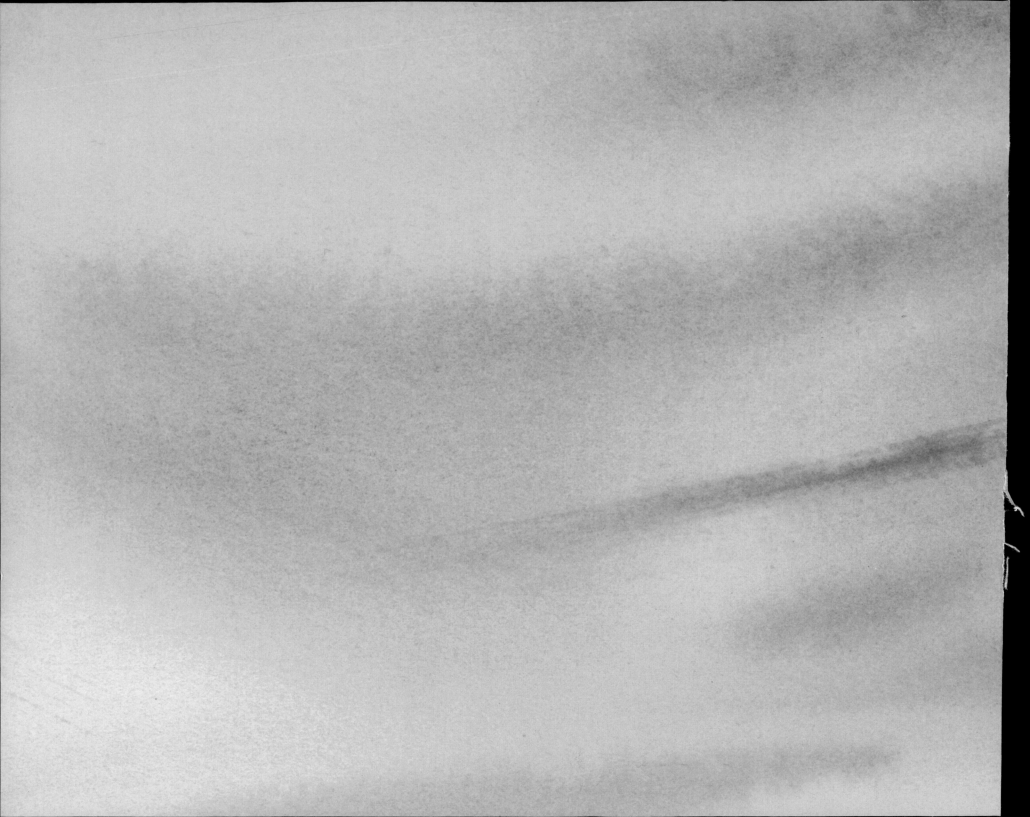